To My Beloved
Child

MEET THE AUTHOR

Tanya Crowley was raised in Yarra Valley, Victoria. Her love of animals and the land led her to a bachelor degree in Agricultural Science. On graduating, she established a local rural store to expand on her father's timber and hardware store. Along side her husband, Ross, she is living out her dream of raising her 3 amazing children on a small block of land. The perfect space to throw the ball for Teddy, the family Labrador, and create new interesting spaces for their comical little family of ducks.

Tanya isn't content in sticking to one thing. Her love of new projects has seen her dabbling in cooking, painting, horse riding, dirt biking, dog breeding, renovating, drumming, and obviously writing! Tanya's most exciting adventure has been discovering the truth of who her Saviour is. Breaking down walls of man-made religion. A lifestyle of constant diving into the unknown of God's world, and re-emerging with a mind transformed by even just one simple new truth from Jesus. And then there's the journey of stewarding that new truth in an every day busy life, without leaving it on the shelf with other bright ideas. The Perfect Plan was birthed from this journey - a life changing experience in itself.

MEET THE ILLUSTRATOR

Perie Whitefield, affectionately named Pear, was raised in a small country town in the Yarra Valley. After completing a diploma of Naturopathy, she went on to complete a bachelor of Health Science in Nutritional Medicine, followed by a post graduate bachelor degree in Primary and Secondary Teaching, Science and Biology. Years of knowledge under her belt soon moved her into teaching Secondary Food Studies. Perie delights in showing teenagers the art of cooking. She guides them in identifying, analysing and understanding food ingredients.

Perie expresses herself through many passions at home. She loves gardening, cooking and eating (of course!), playing with clay, soaking in nature, and adopting random stray animals – a special mention to her well-loved ducks. Perie has been blessed with the skill of painting. Her work reflects the essence of colour, beauty and emotions within all of creation that surrounds her. Perie lives with her wonderful husband and son in a quaint little cottage, not far from where she grew up. A house full of cheeky grins as her husband and son pretend not to notice paint smudges on doors, walls and floors where Perie has passionately absorbed herself in her artwork.

The Perfect Plan

Written and Designed by
Tanya Crowley

Illustrated by
Perie Whitefield

In the beginning there was no war.

It was the start of everything, but there was no war. The Light was good, the dark was good. All was made good, and all was at peace. This was the formation, the creation of a plan.

The plan was everything, but even more than everything was the One who envisioned that plan. The plan was good even as the One who made it was good. The One who made it was there before the beginning, after the end, ever present throughout all time.

He put time in motion, the Sun rose above the land. The Sun shone down on everything in the beginning, revealing it was good. Everything the Sun shone down on was pleasing, just as the Sun itself was pleasing. The Sun reflected the One from the beginning. The One from the beginning revealed everything through the Sun.

The Author of the plan loved everything about His plan. Intricate and sophisticated. Beyond comprehension. As the Author crafted it, every step came to pass. Every word chosen perfectly, every path laid down faultlessly. The Author made the plan for all the nations, His perfect gift to those He loved.

The Creator of the plan wrote His heart and life into the pages. Nations were formed, the genesis of man. His heart beat with their heart; when He took a deep breath, they breathed. Their face, turning to His face, brought life with great depth and richness. Every dawn brought new praise on their lips. When the Sun broke over the horizon, every eye looked to the east in sweet anticipation. Every new day revealed a new revelation of the Maker.

Those who came first, the founders of their nation, were first in creation to speak in response to their Maker. They echoed the Author, building life on His plan. They explored and discovered, giving names to creation. And they were beautiful. Woman and Man.

To hold time where it stands. To paint past into present… but no, not the will of man, but the will of the Creator.

There was another too who loved the plan, fascinated by it, mesmerised. But he didn't understand it. He took a page of that plan and changed it. He saw something good and longed for it, but twisted it and made it his own. He longed to be an author of a master plan, but cared for none of that which was created for man. He thought he could dream up his own plan, a facsimile of the original plan. But the Author held safe the secret to the Master Plan. It would never succeed, this counterfeit plan. It would never work wonders, not even for man.

This other, resplendent, mighty, and courageous had fallen from his beautiful song. Hungry for glory, he polished his plan. He decorated it with marvels from his own hand. He gathered supporters from whence he first came. They worshiped him; they followed him; they played a role in his cruel game. They broke the heart of their Creator when they chose to bathe in another's glory. Now fallen from heaven, their hearts were bound to another's story.

Those first to breathe new life, they held faith and hope in their hands. They lived in wonder and amazement. They nurtured creation in gentle arms. Revelling in the Maker's love, they cherished all the life He breathed into them. They were open in their innocence. They had confidence in His plan. No question on their lips. Nothing concealed, nothing demanded. Every word the Maker spoke revealed a trust that could not be broken. Every step the Maker took established a heart to heart that remained open.

Beloved mankind breathed in fragrances that woke the senses, surrounded by colours of glorious splendour, as they wandered magnificent gardens, always alongside their Creator. They danced along paths He laid down for them. They knew the Father's love intimately and longed for every moment they had with Him. They were made to be cherished. So, to their fullness they were cherished. They watched creation increase in beauty as the Maker continued to bless it. They were created for this glory, and the Father showed such delight in it.

But the other who had fallen, he worked his counterfeit plan. He shaped a place for them and drew them in. They fell right into his hands. They thought they could read this substitute plan. But they weren't created for it, this counterfeit plan. It was tarnished and ugly. It filled them with shame. It made them hide in the dark as they spoke the wrong name. They started naming shadows that would creep in the night. The Creator's heart seemed so distant. His Light, His hand receding from view, as the darkness enveloped them and their song lost its tune.

Creation weeps bitterly in the night.
Once expressing life, but now shame and hiding from sight.
Oh, to turn back time and start again.
Yes, to find shelter from affliction and to turn from this pain.
New thoughts are now binding. New feelings are exposed,
like the nakedness that calls out to be clothed.
Shadows are tormenting, tempting death to take hold.
What a troubled old soul. Back to dust man will go.

But the plan isn't finished. He will surely fight to win.

The One who created the plan, He still loved those groping in the dark. So He spoke to them; He called to them. He drew them out from the shadows, towards His open arms. Then, a sacrifice… a glimpse of One to come. Life was taken from innocence to clothe the naked and fallen ones. To cover up a monumental error? No, a reminder of the Maker's love. Man and woman's effort to hide themselves now exchanged for a gentle reminder. What they encountered here was their first taste of grace poured out from the Almighty Healer.

But the "everything" now seemed to lack splendour. No reflection on the Maker. A new knowledge now gained, it stood between creation and Creator, straining their fellowship with the Maker, but His hand stretched out to entice them. A new page had now turned. Minds torn between Maker and Traitor. There was confusion and deception, and self now stood higher, boastful, and arrogant. The One who formed creation watched the traitor seduce a weakened nation.

But the Maker's strategy was still in place. It would not be denied. The one who first longed to be the other, the thief who no longer loved the Creator, he was written into the original plan, though he didn't know it. He thought he had mastered the secret of his own plan, so he presented it to those across the land. He disguised it with false promises. Backed it up with distorted words and wonders. He recruited the Maker's beloved people, building supporters intended for a far greater purpose. Momentum was now building, full commitment to his plan.

Many from the nations followed this inferior plan. They were deceived. They were celebrated by the thief but forfeited their position with the One who loves. Nations drifted. Feet wandered. Minds tormented with questioning, and hearts ached with grieving. They thirsted, but for what? Their tongues could not be quenched.

But the One from the beginning was always present. He walked through the nations and over the lands. Mankind no longer sought Him; they turned their eyes from Him. But the Maker's heart still longed for them. He pondered His next move and gathered His thoughts. He watched with sorrow as the good turned from colours to a murky grey haze. Shadows surrounded what once shone with beauty. Creation now felt the full weight of death and decay, as mankind fell into the snare of this traitor.

But with such proficiency, such insight, with abundant grace in His heart, He had written new colours in His original plan. He washed out the grey and painted the sky with stunning bright colours that would capture the eye. Here a promise was declared, a reminder of hope for those spared. He looked fondly to one family, whom He saved for the fight. This single family was found worthy. They remained devoted to His plan. They kept sight of it, meditated on it, and held unswerving faith in it. To this faithful family, He had a message. He was setting up a nation that would lead people to His Light.

In a recreation of the beginning, new Light shone through the valleys; Radiating across fields filled with wildflowers, shimmering through crystal clear streams, and penetrating the lush forests that clothed the majestic mountains. Each move of the thief was exposed by that Light. Every fighting move of the thief was consumed with frustration. Blinkered eyes became opened. Hardened hearts beat once again. Hope sparked a new fire amongst those once enslaved from within.

The One who loved all, had a perfect plan from the beginning. He declared war on the enemy for all generations to come. He set in motion what no other man could accomplish. He established a mighty army throughout all time, selecting courageous, faithful soldiers, and equipping them with the finest armour and handcrafted weapons beyond compare.

He wrote the War Plan and put it in the hands of His people. They could soon navigate through the battlefield. Step by step they followed these commands. They memorised them and passed them down through generations. They offered up all that was required of them, sacrificing much for the cause. They learned to lock their eyes on what was to come. There were gentle whispers on the wind, of things long hoped for.

The Mighty One established a royal priesthood, within a mighty nation. He built a connection with them that would last for all time. He raised up kings and princes; He trained up messengers to deliver His commands. He ignited the hearts of princesses, who nurtured the sons and daughters that followed them. He knew what He was doing, and He reigned over everything.

He held His place above all nations, and even royalty bent a knee to Him. They called Him King above all kings and Lord above all lords. They knew Him as trustworthy, and they knew Him as The One. They called Him Father, and they listened to Him like a son.

He then sent word to all, to prepare for His next move. Some moved slowly, but many rushed in. They could see something set before them. They could see the crown of the King.

The King's strategy was perfected as He laid His plans within His royal house. The air carried sweet sounds and wonders as creation breathed and embraced the One to come. He chose someone closest and put everything on the line. He invested all His Kingdom to send out one Man in perfect time. This move was unheard of, and seemed unsafe and unwise. The risk that was taken, too great for man to see through his own eyes.

It was His Son that He sent who had seen the whole plan. The Son knew it intricately yet was willing like no other man. It was His Son who stood amongst His soldiers and experienced all their pain. He walked beside them in their battle and made it His own. He walked shoulder to shoulder as men stumbled forward and picked up their weapons when they tripped and faltered. His face was like the Father, full of love for His own men. He held authority over all creation but walked humbly like other men.

The Son washed away old ways to make way for this new stage. He met His men at the river, refreshing, life-giving water. He buried their old life and set them up for a new fight. No more striving for power, He became the perfect answer. He lifted the weight of the yoke they all carried. The river now consumed all that they gave Him. It flushed away dark things that once held them in bondage. Pain and anguish dealt with at last. Guilt and shame a thing of the past.

The Son spoke of His Father's plan in detail and formed an alliance. His words echoed the Father, establishing a deep trust as He spoke them. He built up an army of soldiers as He walked among them. They varied in skills and training. They continued to falter like all men. But the eyes of the Son, they showed no shame. They shone love and adoration and inflicted no pain. Just a gentle outstretched hand, and they moved on as planned. His strategy was foreign and unexpected, and challenged many commands, but seemed to forge strongholds that were built to last.

Oh, Heir to the throne, Royal Son of the King.
You exchanged robes for your armour and let the battle begin.
Belonging high in your castle but now descended to the battleground.
You are worthy of all honour, but you humbly lay it all down.
Listening for every word from the Father, you wait for every move.
Your steps are a dance in the battle, and your Father's voice is the perfect tune.

The Son's intimacy with the Father brought supreme wisdom to the battleground. Soldiers soon learned by example how to master the Battle Plan. Many clashes with the enemy were met with confidence and skill. They mirrored the Son's movement and sent enemy to the hills. Lost men were found. Broken women were healed. Some cheated death as the Son pulled them out from the enemy's heel. He held children in great esteem and gave them dreams of the future. He recruited new men and restored old men from the lies of the accuser.

But some soldiers took on their own quest, with might and with passion. They laid down their own rules. Through sweat and toil, their armour was fashioned. It was brittle and insufficient for the battle ahead, but to them, impressive and shiny, a glimmer that would turn heads. They presented in good form and knew the right language, but spoke the wrong message. They looked down their noses, judging others around them. They shouted their rules as if they came from the Maker. They kept looking to the heavens, but couldn't see past their own reflection.

The Son challenged the thoughts of those that opposed Him. He spoke only wisdom and sent them off bewildered and moaning. They stewed in their offence; built up their accusations. They turned against the Son of their Maker, as their hearts turned cold. They thought they had authority, but they were pawns in a losing game. They thought they had their enemy, but it was all against their Maker's name.

The enemy formed his army, but royal sword hit enemy ground. The enemy kept on stumbling when the King's army was around. When darkness struck in vengeance, his arrow missed the mark. He was soon to lose his foothold. He was soon to lose his spark. But the battle wasn't over. Enemy focused on his fight. His army was gaining power as he lured others to his side. He gathered his dark knights; He trained them, gave them weapons, and pushed them forward to the fight.

The King watched and waited with pain in His heart. He knew what was happening, but He knew it would pass. The Prince stood at forefront of the battleground. He shielded His army, took the brunt of it, and fell down. Through bloodstained eyes, He looked to the King's chariot; His rescue could be there. But He chose to look to His Father, and the bittersweet pain that they shared. He held the King's war plan, and He knew what to do. He knew of the overflowing joy that His Father had in view. One look at His army, now the battle could be won. He let darkness take Him. His men could only run. They ran in all directions, in despair and such grief. Not realising the strength of the War Plan. Not understanding the truth of who was in defeat.

As soldiers scattered and stumbled, feeling lost and confused, with the darkness falling around them, they felt defeated and bruised. A plan was torn in two and all of heaven could now see. Something was put in motion that would set the nations free. The Son had seen this coming. He had seen this great price to pay. His Father could have taken this bitter cup from Him but chose to love mankind unconditionally. The ultimate sacrifice of all time, the greatest sacrifice heaven and earth could ever see. This Son of the King of all nations gave up His own perfect life, willingly.

The battle had gone deeper, deep behind enemy lines. The Sun had left the heavens; a great darkness enveloped mankind. Both enemy and King's army were blinded in the fight, not knowing what was happening until Truth radiated through the night. Then blinkers were taken off to give them back their clear sight. The enemy and the King's army now came face to face with a new Light.

To the depths of the dark, You have fallen.
Taken the brunt of all sin, You have fallen.
You have given up all for Your army,
and lost Your throne and Your glory for all men.
You lost sight of Your Father who loves you,
for the sake of a Love that would endure.
To die for all undeserving nations,
no greater Love has ever been heard of.

All soldiers who saw beyond the battlefield once again gathered as one army. Each soldier could now see the Author's perfect plan was to defeat enemy on bended knee.

Humble Son had knelt lower than any man would want to be. He chose to follow the Father's plan and nailed it to a tree. This tree was in a glorious garden, where both army and enemy could only marvel at its beauty. There upon that tree was the wisdom for all to see. The soldiers now saw the thief's deception. Now the Father would reveal what He could see.

The Son dwelt in His garden; His army fell to their knees. He had stomped on the enemy of all nations. He cheated death, and offered His gift: to be forever free. The Light shone around Him, revealing One so pure and clean. His face shone like the Father, the deep love radiated from within. The Son had done it all for them when they wanted to flee. He reached a loving hand to them, reassuringly. He showed them no judgement, just love in His eyes. They could now see things more clearly as He showed them the prize.

The King and His Prince, they united again. But before He could go, He had much to say to His men. There wasn't a command, or a push to go forward. He gave them a choice. He never made it a demand. He invited them to freely follow in the rest of the plan, but they would only succeed with the help of His hand. Their own page in the Master Plan relied completely on the Son's sacrifice; each debt paid in full, so the King could complete His Masterpiece.

The Prince and the King left a Book of Instructions. This Book laid out old rules, but highlighted the new ones. It portrayed the heart of the Prince which led to His Father. It ignited a spark in the hearts of the soldiers and gave them new life, and a Helper to guide them.

This Helper was often gentle and quiet, but embodied the fullness of the King and Prince. He spoke whispers alongside the new army. He comforted them, guided them, and spoke life-changing truths to them. The Helper received words from the Son, and formed them into dreams that spoke into the future. He shone light on the Book of instructions, giving meaning to every word on the pages. The soldiers soon delighted in their Helper, as their minds intently locked onto their Saviour.

They now had a mission, to send word throughout the land: "The enemy has lost his authority and is now in your hands". They shared what they'd learned from the Saviour, their friend. They shared that He'd given them the King's signet ring. The King's army received authority to push out the enemy forces. When the thief tried to deceive again, the soldiers came with their horses.

Oh, mighty army, bring forth your song.
Lift your voices to the skies.
Lift your swords to the heavens, and strike fear in your enemy's eyes.
Your strength is unequalled when you stand by the King's side.
When you fix your eyes on the heavens,
you conquer death and reveal the lies.
There's freedom set before you,
as you reveal what's in the Prince's hands.
You hold the keys to the Kingdom
when you speak words from the Master Plan.

As the King revealed His glory to the loyal army on the ground, they soon learned to leave their belongings behind as they relied completely on the King's plan. The Prince gave the Helper some armour, much lighter than before. The Helper then gave it to the soldiers to equip them in their mission to restore. They now moved swifter, stronger, and more directly in their new identity. They now had a vision revealed to them that would spread word as far as the seas.

The soldiers entered into a deeper communion, with the Helper who guided them, the Son who saved them, and the Father who loved them. There was talk of a banquet that was being set before them, a banquet for many from a King who adored them. But before they could sit at this great, royal table, the soldiers gathered together to celebrate. They gathered together with wine in one hand, breaking bread with others who remembered His plan. There was a sacrifice they could celebrate, and the King celebrated this One too. A sacrifice that built perfect family, for all eternity renewed.

The King, the Prince, and the Helper looked on with pride at the treasures they found. They formed and they moulded. They polished and shined. They made heaven's delight in their image as mankind. They saw perfect soldiers from the beginning of time and called them into being with a perfect plan, in perfect time. They brushed off the dirt and polished the armour and stood their dear soldiers in the King's royal line.

The soldiers stood like lampstands, shining bright like their Saviour. They learned to be humble, just to stand with their Maker. They stumbled and fell but rose to their feet. They were called by the Creator to win battles and never retreat. They looked to the heavens, to where they belonged. They called to the Father, all in one song "Bring Heaven to earth, and Your glory will come. Your glory on earth, as Your will be done".

Sing praises from the mountains. Sing out "Glory to the King".
Bring Heaven to all earth before the banquet begins.
Crimson water pours like wine; cleansing water covers the Vine.
Something broken, now repaired when Son claimed back His heritage.
Earth in mourning is now rejoicing, as life is given back to creation.
So freely given, now freely received.
All glory to the Son for what He achieved!

While sitting by His Father, the Son gazed out. He watched His beloved army with deep joy in His heart. He knew them as family. He knew them by name. The Father whispered the secrets of their hearts without shame. He knew each soldier's song, and He sang their new tune. Heavenly creations gathered before Him to take part and be moved. He created the heavens, the earth, and the seas. He created it all for mankind, and motioned soldiers to agree.

The King and the Prince and the Helper combined led more people to freedom than ever in time. They commissioned their army and built on their forces, with one joy in mind, to be forever united. They planned a perfect new creation. A new place to call home. The Father's beloved children would live forever as one family, in perfect peace, in perfect love. Eternity with the Father who created all things; Eternity with the Helper who guided their paths; a Son in all glory would humbly stand side by side, forever with mankind.

The King and the Prince set a table before them. All elements carefully placed for an extravagant feast. Food of new colours, new flavours of Heaven. Glistening crystal filled with new wine from the Master. Every magnificently crafted seat was placed with intention. This love poured out, not yet fully comprehended. Yet would one day be received in its fullness…Yes, would one day be received in all its fullness!

The King and the Prince looked at the banquet table and then smiled at each other. Every place reserved for His soldiers had been paid in full—redeemed in full by His blood.

… and that there is The Perfect Plan. A mission so perfectly accomplished!

Published in Australia in 2022 by Tanya Crowley

Text and Cover Design Copyright © Tanya Crowley, 2022.
Illustrations copyright © Perie Whitefield, 2022.

The moral rights of both Author and illustrator have been asserted.

Cataloguing-in-Publication data is available from the National Library of Australia.

ISBN 978-0-6454836-0-4